txt me
baby
[1 more
time]

THIS IS A CARLTON BOOK

Text and design copyright © 2001 Carlton Books Limited

This edition published by Carlton Books Limited 2001
20 Mortimer Street, London W1T 3JW

A CIP catalogue for this book is available from the British Library.

ISBN 1 84222 396 8

Printed and bound in Italy

Editorial Manager: Venetia Penfold
Art Director: Penny Stock
Project Editor: Zia Mattocks
Text and design: Terry Burrows
Production Controller: Janette Davis

txt me baby [1 more time]

CARLTON
BOOKS

contents

WotsGoinOn?

6 **what's goin' on?**

RURdy2GtWlvTTxt?

16 **are you ready to get with the text**

JstALt1Crsh

26 **just a little crush**

HtDts

32 **hot dates**

F1ngOrTR1Thng?

38 **fling or the real thing?**

RmntcF0l

44 **romantic fool**

Hrtbrk&SRw

50 **heartbreak and sorrow**

HPyNdng

58 **happy ending**

what's goin' on?

Your cool guide to get you started on the ride.

It's funny to think that ten years ago hardly anyone had a mobile phone. Those that did were rich, famous and had MASSIVE biceps — some of those things were the size of a small fridge! Now, of course, EVERYONE has one. We've come to depend on them. Where would most of us be without one? Sad, lonely and lost, that's where.

But you can do more with a mobile phone than just talk. A few years ago some clever geeks came up with the brainy idea of letting mobile phones transmit little messages to one another. In most cases, they thought, it would be used for boring suity-type things like arranging meetings. Little did they know they were about to unleash a revolution.

Whether it was called SMS, GSM, G-mail or plain old TEXT MESSAGING, it quickly became a phenomenally popular and rather cool way of communicating. In fact, over 500 million people all over the world now regularly send and receive text messages.

Why has the world gone text crazy?

Maybe it's because text messaging has all the usual advantages of a mobile phone without turning you into an embarrassing public menace. Let's be honest, nobody likes to be stuck on a train next to someone braying loudly into their phone. Texting, on the other hand, is discreet. A quiet bleep or sexy vibration is all it takes to let you know that a message has arrived.

Texting is also cheaper than making a regular phone call: each message costs only a few pence. And when have you ever managed to phone up a friend to arrange a meeting place without it turning into a half-hour chat on the latest hot gossip that's doing the rounds?

OK, enough of the sensible reasons, mostly we text because it's FUN. But it's also practical fun. Do you start to feel tongue-tied when you want to tell your partner how you feel about them? Texting over ILUvU should do the trick. Have you got a crush and a phone number but are not sure how you can take it a stage further? Try DUWnt2GoOut2nite?

Not everyone loves texting. Some academics fear that it may affect literacy. As Dr Ken Lodge of the University of East Anglia claims: 'It could restrict people's abilities to communicate ... inevitably it'll affect the way they talk to each other.'

How does it all work?

Like the Internet, text messaging has evolved it's own system of language and grammar. You can take a combination of three approaches to sending your own text messages: ACRONYMS, VOWEL-DROPS and EMOTICONS.

An ACRONYM is a made-up word where each letter represents the first letter of a another word. For example, PCM can be used as shorthand for PLEASE CALL ME. Acronymns like this can save you loads of time, but if you use them make sure that they are common currency: it's no use texting

FADATAPATMWCGOTAC

if your mate doesn't know that you mean

W🚓TCH IT!

Even the most expensive mobile phones have only a limited room to store messages. When it gets filled up you may not be able to receive new messages until you have made space. Therefore it's a good idea to get into the habit of deleting your unwanted messages.

FANCY A DRINK AND THEN A PIZZA AND THEN MAYBE WE CAN GO ON TO A CLUB.

VOWEL-DROPPING is a safer way to text. No surprises here, this means leaving out most of the vowels from your messages. For added clarity, it's a good idea to start each new word with a capital letter. Some texters also like to leave a space between words, but although this can clarify meaning it also takes

11

up extra time and space. But the choice is yours – nobody's going to give you an F in the world of text messaging. (Well they might, but that's an altogether different story!)

Another popular shortcut is to play with phonetics. Instead of writing out FOR, you can use the number 4; instead of YOU, the letter U will do nicely. So LET'S GET TOGETHER abbreviates to LtsGt2gthr. You can also shorten key words: LOVE is transformed into Luv; WITH becomes WiV. Another common practice is to show double letters within a word as a single capital letter – SORRY might be shown as SRy. You get the picture, right?

The final idea we'll look at here is the EMOTICON. This system of symbols emerged in the early days of the Internet as a way of conveying emotion in text. Typed words can easily be misleading on their own. Are you being funny or sarcastic? It's sometimes hard to tell. You can of course emphasize some words by TYPING THEM IN CAPITALS but

W TCH IT!

Emoticon symbols maybe creative and fun to use but they can also be a bit of a pain. Unlike computer keyboards, mobile phones don't have enough pads for all of the punctuation marks. Instead they are all contained within a special screen that you have to 'click' your way through.

HOT T/PS

The first and last rules of text messaging are simple: THERE ARE NO RULES. Texting is all about effective communication. As long as the person receiving your message can understand your acronyms and abbreviations then anything you choose to send is good.

that's likely to be interpreted as shouting,

which is a little rude. A more subtle alternative

is to create little faces using the punctuation

marks found on your phone's keypad. The

most common emoticon is the good old SMILEY

face. You can create this using a colon,

dash and closed brackets – just like this :—).

If you turn it around by 90 degrees clockwise

you'll see the effect.

There are numerous other possibilities.
For example, a great text-messaging game is
to send mystery emoticons to your friends and
let them guess the meaning. Or why not try the
FAMOUS NAMES GAME?

Question: Who is this?

@@@@:-)

Answer: Marge Simpson

So there it is. Welcome to the rather
fabulous world of text messaging. It can be
as serious, stupid, creative, practical or fun as
you want it to be. As with everything else, the
choice is yours. So what are you waiting for?
LtsGtTxtng.

are you ready to get with the text?

The basic tools you need to get yourself up and running.

As with any other language, you need to equip yourself with the basics before you can get down to serious business. Let's start with a list of REALLY simple expressions – the sort of thing that everybody who texts should know.

HOT TIPS

Some of this might seem a bit inscrutable and weird at first, but stick with it – the more you text the easier it gets.

2	To/two/too
2day	Today
2moro	Tomorrow
4	For
4WIW	For what it's worth
@	At
AAM	As a matter of fact
AFAIC	As far as I'm concerned
AFAIK	As far as I know
AKA	Also known as
ASAP	As soon as possible
ATB	All the best
ATM	At the moment
B	Be
BBFN	Bye bye for now
B/C	Because
BCNU	Be seeing you
B4	Before
BFN	Bye for now
BRB	Be right back
BTW	By the way

RURdy2GtwivTTxt?

Bwd	Backward
BYKT	But you knew that
C	See
CMIIW	Correct me if I'm wrong
CU	See you
CUL8r	See you later
CYA	See you (see ya)
Doin	Doing
EOL	End of line (that's final)
Esp	Especially
FAQ	Frequently asked questions
FITB	Fill in the blank
F2T	Free to talk?
FWIW	For what it's worth
FYI	For your information
Gd	Good
GG	Good game
Gonna	Going to
HAND	Have a nice day
HTH	Hope this helps
HUH	Have you heard?

HOT T*I*PS

*Combine the sounds of letters and numbers to create new words or personal identities. For example, the word GREAT can be texted as **Gr8**.*

H2	How to
H8	Hate
IAC	In any case
IC	I see
IDK	I don't know
IK	I know
IMHO	In my humble opinion
IMNSHO	In my not so humble opinion
IOW	In other words
IYSS	If you say so
L8	Late
L8r	Later
LMK	Let me know
LOL	Laughs out loud
Luv	Love
M8	Mate

RURdy2GtWivTTxt?

M80	Matey
MYOB	Mind your own business
NE	Any
NE 1	Anyone
NEtm	Anytime
Neva	Never
No 1	No one
OIC	Oh, I see
Pls	Please
Ppl	People
R	Are
Re	Regarding
ROTFL	Rolls on the floor laughing

WOW!

Much to the annoyance of President Joseph Estrada, the people of the Philippines have taken to texting in a very big way. In fact, he believed that rumours and rude jokes about him were being sent by rebel forces in an effort to destabilize his administration.

20

RU?	Are you?
SpK	Speak
Sry	Sorry
Tho	Though
ThnQ	Thank you
Thru	Through
Thx	Thanks
TNX	Thanks
U	You
U@	(Where are) you at?
UOK	You OK?
UR	You are
Usu	Usually
W/	With
Wan2	Want to
WerRU	Where are you?
W/o	Without
W8	Wait
W8ng	Waiting
YM	You mean
YR	Yeah, right!

♥ RURdy2GtWivTTxt? ♥

Make a show of your feelings!

Now let's take a look at a handful of the most commonly used emoticons. These can be used to tell people exactly how you feel, either in terms of your mood or as a curt response to a previous message.

The basic idea is pretty simple. In the original smiley face, a colon represent eyes, a dash is the nose and a closed bracket is the smiling mouth. Other letters or punctuation

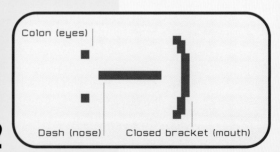

Colon (eyes)

Dash (nose)   Closed bracket (mouth)

marks can be added to produce different effects. For example, a closed bracket can be a sad, drooping mouth; a semi-colon a winking eye; lower-case letter d a baseball cap. You're limited only by your imagination.

:−)	Happy
:−))	Very happy
:−(	Sad
:−((	Very sad
:−||	Angry
:'−(	Crying
%−\	Confused
:−>	Devilish grin
;−>	Devilish wink
[:−(	Frowning
:−/	Frustrated
:−*	Blowing a kiss
:−D	Loud Laugh

C👓OL STUFF

*Use emoticons to share your mood or provide a succinct reaction to a message. The question **UOK?** (Are you alright?) could perhaps be answered with :-[(I'm really sad) or :-| (I'm not talking to you).*

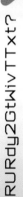

:-|	Not talking
:O	Loud yell
:-@	Screaming
:-o	Shocked
:'-O	Shocked and upset
:-p	Tongue-in-cheek
d:-)	Hats off – great idea
:-S	Lying
:-%	So-so, 50-50
:-$	Secret
:-[	Feeling down
:->>	Huge grin
:-))))	REALLY happy
{}	No comment

:-&	Tongue-tied
:-X	Big wet kiss
M:-)	I salute you
:-#	Lips are sealed
(:-...	Heart-broken
:-e	Disappointed
:-t	Upset and pouting
;(	Cheer up
;)	Smirk
:|	Hmmm ...
:}	What?!
8-)	Wearing glasses
B-)	Wearing shades
:c	Very unhappy
:Y	Whispered aside
;?	Wry remark
:?	Licking lips
:~)	Yum, yum
:")	A bit embarrassed
X-(	Mad with rage
;}	Leer

RURdy2GtWivTTxt?

25

just a little crush

fancy someone and want to get to know them better? All it can take is one little text message.

Now let's turn our attention to oiling the wheels of romance. That can only mean one thing — FLIRTING. In fact, it could have been what text messaging was made for, especially if you're a little on the shy side. You can be wry, clever, sassy, sexy, mysterious or full-on.

TCBYLD
This could be your lucky day

TCBYLN
This could be your lucky night

UHvABf?
Do you have a boyfriend?

There are loads of romantic symbols that you can use when texting love matters. A KISS is represented by the traditional X, (or *X*) and a HUG is *H*. A commonly used emoticon for HUGS AND KISSES is [()]:** . The most common symbol used to represent the HEART is <3 (it's actually supposed to be a beating heart).

JstALtlCrsh

UHvAGf?

> Do you have a girlfriend?

GW?

> Guess who?

WGYMN?

> Who gave you my number?

>-::-D

> I've been struck by cupid's arrow

:-6

> Losing sleep over you, baby

@}>-,-——

> A rose for you

CnlFlrtWivU?

> Can I flirt with you?

(*_*)

> Goggle-eyed for you

RUSmart?

A mysterious message arrives. All it says is:
HAY&M? **What do you make of it?**
a) How are you and Mum?
b) Do you have any yams and mangos?
c) How about you and me?

Most
likely C.
Unless you have
some odd
friends!

UWan2Gt2gthr?

You want to get together?

IAD

It's a date

INoSumwerC1WeC1dMt

I know somewhere cool we could
meet

ULkALtLkMyNxtBf

You look a lot like my next
boyfriend

IfHeDsntShwUplmHre

If he doesn't show up, I'm here

HrsYrChnc2Gt2NoMe

Here's your chance to get to
know me

DntUNoMeFrmSumwer

Don't you know me from
somewhere?

You could be anyone

When you send a message, unless the receiver knows your number they will have no idea who you are. Sometimes it's nice to give a clue; sometimes an air of mystery is more fun. Other times you might want to have a laugh. Check out these emoticons.

:-	I'm a man
:-)8-	I'm a man
>-	I'm a woman
:-)3>-	I'm a woman
O:-)	Smiling angel
O,-)	Winking angel
((Y))	Big lady
:-[	Vampire
=:-)	Punk rocker
+:-)	The pope
(:<)	Donald Duck
:-)#	Man with a beard
:-)##	Man with a long beard

:-)#3	Woman with beard
:-#	Man with moustache
:-)J	Surfer
:-)o->	Suity type
:-.)	Madonna/Marilyn Monroe
:-+	Babe with too much lipstick
:----)	Liar (Pinnochio)
:------)	BIG liar
:-[x>	Count Dracula
::-)	Four-eyes
:-~)	Someone with a cold
:::-)	The Elephant Man
:>)	Big nose
:@)	Pig face
:-{}	Lipstick lover
:-)>	Man with a goatee
D)	Wearing a crash helmet
<:-))	Stupid but happy
<:-(	Sad dunce
=:x	Bunny
@-)	Smiling cyclops

True(ish) Love Stories

Part 1

It started in a coffee bar. Brendan had fancied Cat for ages, but the time had never been right to make a move. Now she was here, probably waiting for her mates. It was too good to be true. Brendan picked up his phone and began texting.

B: GW?   (Guess who?)
C: :- or >   (Male or female?)
B: SoVS   (Someone very special)
B: ;-] :-#   (*Winks and blows a kiss*)
C: UHvABshyMustsh?
                        (You have a bushy moustache?)
B: NO :-*;   (No, I was blowing you a kiss!)
C: ThtsVryFrwrd   (That's very forward of you!)
B: :-$ (I have a secret)
C: ?   (What's that?)
B: IfncyU   (I fancy you)
C: (o_o)   (I'm shocked!)
B: Wan2NoWhoIam?
                        (Want to know who I am?)
C: OK   (All right)
B: LkAcrSTROm   (Look across the room)

JstALtlCrsh

31

hot dates

You've broken the ice, but what happens next is up to you.

You know you're smitten, but how do you move things up a notch without getting tongue-tied or plain embarrassed? Right now you don't have to say a word – just trust the text.

HtDts

UFnCMe?

Do you fancy me?

IFnCU

I fancy you

:-)(-: +

Feel like a snog?

HaBaBWan2GtLcky?

Hey baby, want to get lucky?

GetYaCotUvePuLd

Get your coat, you've pulled!

HwDoULkMeSoFa?

How do you like me so far?

SoHwMlDoin?

So … how am I doing?

OKYLDo

OK, you'll do

PdnMeIsUrStTkn?

Pardon me, is your seat taken?

StndStLIWnt2PckUUp

Stand still, I want to pick you up

DUB1vNF8?

Do you believe in fate?

IveCum2StE1Ur<3

I've come to steal your heart

IsItHtNHrOrIsItJstU?

Is it hot in here or is it just you?

IDdntNoAng1sF1wSoLo

I didn't know angels flew so low

RntUMyB1ndDt42nite?

Aren't you my blind date for tonight?

WrHvUBEnALMyLfe?

Where have you been all my life?

AML

All my love

BBSS

Be back soon sweetheart

CSThnknAbtU

Can't stop thinking about you

The dating game

OK, the preliminaries are out of the way. Now it's time to get down to the serious business of dating. Here are some practical text tips to help you on your way.

WSWM
Where shall we meet?

WenDoWeMEt?
When do we meet?

2day
Today

2moro
Tomorrow

WATCH IT!

If you use texting for getting dates or meeting people, exercise a bit of caution, especially where relative strangers are involved. Keep your initial meetings to public places and, if possible, let a friend or member of your family know your plans. Better safe than sorry.

ADN

Any day now

ASAP

As soon as possible

ATM

At the moment

CWYL

Chat with you later

L8rBaB

Later, baby

DUWnt2GoOut2nite

Do you want to go out tonight?

ETA

Estimated time of arrival

LMK

Let me know

MED

Immediately

Sec

Second

Soons

As soon as

W84Me@

Wait for me at …

WerRU

Where are you?

Spk@UL8r

Speak to you later

HtDts

CU2nite@8

See you tonight at eight

YrPlcOrMne?

Your place or mine

GnaMakUAnOFrUCntRfs

Gonna make you an offer you

can't refuse

ILBTher4U

I'll be there for you

NEdU2nite

Need you tonight

NEd2CU2nite

Need to see you tonight

ItsNwOrNvr

It's now or never

CBS

Call back soon

TBC

To be confirmed

TBA

To be announced

GGN

Got to go now

PlsDntGo

Please don't go

U+Me=Luv

You + Me = LOVE

True(ish) Love Stories

Part 2

Cat looked over to see a grinning Brendan the other side of the coffee bar. But at that same moment her mates trooped in. If they didn't leave straight away they'd miss the start of the movie. Cat glanced over at Brendan, gave a wry smile and shrugged her shoulders. Was that the end of the story?

B: **GW?**   (Guess who?)

C: **UAgn**   (You again)

B: **IThtIdLstU4Evr** (I thought I'd lost you forever)

B: **>:->**   (*remark made with a devilish grin*)

C: **:-D <L>**   (Very funny! *Laughs*)

B: **RUOK**   (Are you alright?)

C: **1dafl**   (Wonderful)

B: **JstLkU**   (Just like You!)

C: **Stp *^_^***   (Stop, you're making me blush!)

B: **Wan2Gt2gthr**   [Do you want to get together?]

C: **%-| IDK**   [*Confused.* I don't know]

B: **Y? UKUW2**   [Why? You know you want to]

B: **:-)**   [*Winks knowingly*]

C: **IDK CBL8rOK**   [I don't know. Call back later, OK?]

B: **L8rBaB :-))**   (Later baby! *Massive grin*)

37

fling or the real thing?

Ah, when love is new ... there's nothing like it. A ringing phone, a postman's knock, a message bleep and the heart starts racing. But really, it's all about getting to know someone, which a lot of time can just mean chatting away about any old rubbish.

AWHFY	Are we having fun yet?
Bf	Boyfriend
BOC	But of course
BTTP	Back to the point
UBsy?	Are you busy?
CB	Call back
CHWUR	See how you are

Texting can save your life. On Valentine's Day 2001 holiday-maker Rebecca Fyfe and 17 others were stranded in a boat off the coast of Indonesia after an engine failure. They were rescued after she texted her boyfriend, Nick Hodgson, back in England, who was able to alert coastguards in Southeast Asia.

FlngOrTRIThng?

CHUR	See how you are
CUBL8r	Call you back later
DnUTnk	Do you think?
DK	Don't know
DTRT	Do the right thing
DUCWIC	Do you see what I see?
FncyAShg?	Fancy a shag?
GA	Go ahead
Gf	Girlfriend
GMTA	Great minds think alike
GTBOS	Glad to be of service
H&K	Hugs and kisses
HH	Holding hands

HOYEW	Hanging on your every word
HSIK	How should I know?
HTEI	Hope this explains it
HTH	Hope this helps
HUH	Have you heard?
IDGI	I don't get it
IDTS	I don't think so
IKT	I know that
ILU	I love you
ILY	I love you
INT	I'll never tell
IOU	I owe you
IOU 1	I owe you one
IWIK	I wish I knew
IXU	I love you
IXXXXU	I love you lots
KOTL	Kiss on the lips
KWIM	Know what I mean
HK	Hot kiss
IWBNI	It would be nice if ...
JAM	Just a minute

FlngOrTRlThng?

HOT T I PS

Overcome with romantic thoughts while sitting at your desk? Everyone loves flowers, so why not send him or her a lovely rose? Or even a dozen?

@}>-'-,--
12X---<--@

JAS	Just a second
LBF	Let's be friends
LJBF	Let's just be friends
LTNH	Long time no hear
LTNC	Long time no see
LOL	Lots of love
LOL	Laughs out loud
LULAB	Love you like a brother
LULAS	Love you like a sister
Luv	Love
NAGI	Not a good idea
NIAA	No idea at all
NQA	No questions asked

FIngOrTRIThng?

PDA	Public display of affection
RFC	Request for comments
RUF2T	Are you free to talk?
RUOK	Are you OK?
SVS	Someone very special
SWAK	Sealed with a kiss
TC	Take care
TCB	Taking care of business
TCL	Take care, love
TLC	Tender loving care
URVSxy	You are very sexy
Wadya	What do you ...?
WerUBin	Where have you been?
Wot	What?

Hw2MprSAWmn: LuvHr,CmfrtHr,XXXHr&RspctHr.

How to impress a woman: Love her, comfort her, kiss her and respect her.

Hw2MprSAMan:TrnUpNkd.BrngBEr.

How to impress a man: Turn up naked. Bring beer.

True(ish) Love Stories

Part 3

Brendan knew he was getting through to Cat. One more call should seal the deal.

B:	**JstMe**	(It's just me)
C:	**WDYW**	(What do you want)
B:	**IWT**	(I was thinking)
B:	**HwBout2nite**	(How about tonight?)
C:	**WAI**	(What about it?)
B:	**NEthngDoin**	(Anything doing?)
C:	**IWMHT**	(I'm washing my hair tonight!)
B:	**ICdHlp**	(I could help)
C:	**:@**	(It's true, I swear!)
B:	**:*-(2moro?**	(I'm devastated. Tomorrow?)
C:	**:-**	[*Still can't make up mind*]
B:	**ILTkUSmwerGr8**	
		[I'll take you somewhere great]
C:	**KT**	[Keep talking]
B:	**ULkItlianFOd?**	[You like Italian food?]
C:	**OK IBT**	[OK, I'll be there]
B:	**:-)))))))**	[*Really happy*]
B:	**MEt@8?**	[Meet at eight?]
C:	**COl**	[Cool!]

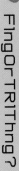

FlngOrTRIThng?

romantic fool

Your head is in the clouds. Your mind's on another planet. What's happening? It must be love.

Where words of love are concerned, texting is just the best. And everyone's a winner: now you no longer have to nauseate your friends and family with cute talk and pet names. It's a virtual universe just made for two.

BK
> Big kiss

F2F
> Face to face

HITULTILuvU?
> Have I told you lately that I love you?

IC**WenUXMe
> I see stars when you kiss me

HOT T🌶PS

By the time you've got to this stage, your names are certain to be programmed into each other's phones, so save yourself some time – you don't need to worry about ending messages with your identity.

ILUM&MED
> I love you more and more each day

JTM
> Je t'aime

LUWAM<3
> Love you with all my heart

URAQT
> You are a cutie

SWALK
> Sent with a loving kiss

TMIY
> Take me I'm yours

U2MeREvrythng
> You to me are everything

WLUStLLuvMe2moro?
> Will you still love me tomorrow?

GBH
> Great big hug

GBH&K
> Great big hug and kiss

RmntcFOI

45

GBH&KCB

Great big hug and kiss coming back

K

Kiss on the cheek

XXXXXXXXX

Very big (and long) kiss

KB

Kiss back

KOTC

Kiss on the cheek

MlUrSgnfcntOthr?

Am I your significant other?

MAY

Mad about you

VH

Virtual hug

:—*

Blowing a kiss

<X

Sloppy wet kiss

Bf: MlYr1st?

Boyfriend: Am I your first?

Gf: UCldB,ULkFmlr

Girlfriend: You could be, you look familiar.

ImADctd2U

I'm addicted to you

Alwys&4evr

Always and forever

CntGtEnufOfUBaB

Can't get enough of you, baby

CntW82CU2nite

Can't wait to see you tonight

4evrInLuv

Forever in love

HldMeClsBaB

Hold me close, baby

HplSlyDvotd2U

Hopelessly devoted to you

IDntDsrvU ...

I don't deserve you ...

... OrMaBIDo

... or maybe I do

StaWivMe2nite

Stay with me tonight

IgotUBbe

I got you babe

ImT14U

I'm the one for you

MakThsANite2Rmba

Make this a night to remember

SoInLuvWivU

So in love with you

And for the REAL smooth talkers ...

Over the centuries, poets and writers have had their say on the perennial matter of LURVE.

HwDoILuvThE?LtMeCntTWys

> How do I love thee? Let me count the ways [Browning]

UShdHvASftrPLwThnMy<3

> You should have a softer pillow than my heart [Byron]

LuvConqrsAL&We2SCmb2Luv

> Love conquers all, and we too succumb to love [Virgil]

4Luv&Buty&DliteTherIsNoDethNrChnge

> For love, and beauty, and delight, there is no death nor change [Shelley]

ShLICmprThE2ASMrsDy? ThouRtMrLvly&MrTmprt

> Shall I compare thee to a summer's day? Thou art more lovely and more temperate [Shakespeare]

2CHrWs2LuvHr,LuvBtHr&Luv4evr

> To see her was to love her, love but her, and love forever [Burns]

Part 4

True(ish) Love Stories

Although it had taken persistence, Brendan quickly won Cat over. Their first date went like a dream – something really clicked between them. Later that night, just as she was about to go to sleep, Cat's phone gave off a quiet bleep.

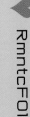

B: **HiSxy**   (Hi sexy)
C: **UOK?**   (Are you alright?)
B: **InHvn**   (In heaven)
B: **:( )**   (I feel like talking all night)
C: **WsThtAYwn?**   (Was that a yawn?)
B: **NO! :-X**   (No! *Blows a kiss*)
C: **ICBYJDT**   (I can't believe you just did that!)
C: **:-/\/\/**   (*Double-sided slap*)
B: **ThtHrt!**   (That hurt)
C: **LMKIB**   [Let me kiss it better]
C: **I***   [*Kisses with eyes closed*]
B: **Wow! :-)<*3**   [Wow! *My heart is pounding*]
C: **ThtBtr?**   [That better?]
B: **Mmmmm**   [Mmmmmm!]
C: **SlpTght**   [Sleep tight]
B: **:-)))))))**   [*Really happy*]

49

heartbreak and sorrow

The course of true love never did run smooth ...

... well that's what Mr Shakespeare reckoned and, let's be honest, he knew a thing or two about romance. So, what do you say when it all goes pear-shaped, you need a pithy put-down, or you just want to let off a bit of steam?

IWntBSDWivU
I wouldn't be seen dead with you

IWMHT
I'm washing my hair tonight

IWMHT&EON
I'm washing my hair tonight and every other night

50

HOT T**I**PS

Many of us have a confidence crisis when facing confrontation. That needn't be the case with text. Don't be afraid to clear the air – just go for it!

ILCUInMyDrms...IflEt2Mch ChEz

> I'll see you in my dreams ... if I eat too much cheese

ItsAShmeUrPrntsDntPrcts SafSx

> It's a shame your parents didn't practice safe sex

NIYWTLPITW

> Not if you were the last person in the world

SIJLIAC

> Sorry, I just lapsed into a coma

PYMIGBOYM

> Put your mind in gear before opening your mouth

RUKDng?

> Are you kidding?

UrPrOfEnfThtICnTkAJk

> Your proof enough that I can take a joke

Q:YWntUMndYrOwnBsnS?
A:UveGtNoMnd&GtNoBsnS
Question: Why won't you mind own own business?
Answer: You've got no mind and got no business.

Hrtbrk&SRw

WTHDTTM

What the hell does that mean?

SUNo1ILTY

Shut up, no one is listening to you

DoSmSoulSrchng.UMghtJst
Fnd1 Do some soul searching. You
might just find one

TYVLYWEL

Thank you very little, you're
welcome even less

MnRLkLefnts.ILk2Lk@Thm
BtWdntWnt2Own1

Men are like elephants: I like to
look at them but wouldn't want
to own one

URLkACrA1rm.UMkALtOfNse
BtNo1PysAnyATntn

You're like a car alarm. You make
a lot of noise but no one pays
any attention

In short ...

But when words fail, you just need something quick and simple. Better make it something smart.

AYM?	Are you mental?
BOAD	Bog off and die!
CFD	Call for discussion
CIfICr	See if I care
CIO	Cut it out
EOD	End of discussion
FCOL	For crying out loud
GAL	Get a life
GL	Get lost
GOOML	Get out of my life
GOWI	Get on with it
HHOS	Ha ha, only serious!
ITSTBF	Is that supposed to be funny?
ITYLE	It took you long enough
KISS	Keep it simple, stupid
KMA	Kiss my arse
LMA	Leave me alone

Hrtbrk&SRw

LTBF	Learn to be funny
MA	My arse!
MYOB	Mind your own business
NOYB	None of your business
NRN	No reply necessary
NRNOE	No reply necessary, or expected
OTL	Out to lunch
PM	Pardon me!
OMG	OH MY GOD!
ONNTA	Oh no, not this again
PITA	Pain in the arse
PO	Piss off!
QI	Quit it!
RB	Reality bypass?
RFD	Request for discussion
SOHF	Sense of humour failure
SI	Shut it!
SLS	So last season
SU	Shut up!
SWYP	So what's your problem?
TAH	Take a hint

Hrtbrk&SRw

54

TNWIS	That's not what I said
TMI	Too much information
TWYT	That's what you think
TYLE	Took you long enough
WALOR	What a load of rubbish
WOWFU	Witless one-word follow-up
WTH	What the hell
WYP	What's your point?
WYSOH	Where's your sense of humour?
XCM	Excuuuuuuuse me!
YPB	Your point being?
YGTBK	You've got to be kidding
YHL	You have lost
YHBW	You have been warned
YOYO	You're on your own

Hrtbrk&SRw

☺

INoUDntNd2UsTltPprCozGdMdUSchAPrfctRs

I know you don't need to use toilet paper
because God made you such a perfect arse.

Say it with symbols

They say that a picture paints a thousand words. Why not make yours a face to remember?

:—e	Very disappointed
(:—/	Very sad
:*(	In tears
>:—<	Mad
>:—<<	REALLY mad
@%&$%	*********!! (expletives deleted)
%—6	Braindead
(:—...	Brokenhearted
(l—(	Good grief!
8^(	Displeased
:—C	VERY displeased
:—(*)	You make me sick!
('^)	Looking away
:—p	Sticks out tongue
:—8(	Condescending stare
3—<	Up yer bum!
::—	THE FINGER

Part 5

True(ish) Love Stories

By this time Cat and Brendan had been going out for several months. Tonight they were supposed to be meeting at the coffee bar at eight. It was now nine fifteen and there was no sign of Brendan. Cat had waited long enough. She stormed out. When she got home she picked up her phone.

C:	**WWerU@**	(Where were you?)
B:	**SryLuv**	(Sorry love)
C:	**LuvMA**	(Love, my arse!)
C:	**YDdntUCL**	(Why didn't you call?)
B:	**CdntGtASgnl**	(Couldn't get a signal)
B:	**ITrd**	(I tried)
C:	**IDBU**	(I don't believe you)
C:	**WGO**	(What's going on?)
B:	**SryIFrgt**	(Sorry, I forgot)
B:	**MI4Gvn**	(Am I forgiven?)
C:	**NO**	(No)
B:	**IMIU2U**	(I'll make it up to you)
C:	**YR**	(Yeah, right!)
B:	**Pls**	(Please?)
C:	**:-|**	(*Refuses to talk anymore*)

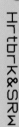

57

happy ending

C'mon, you can't sulk forever! It's time to kiss and make up. After all, everyone loves a happy ending, don't they?

The best bit about falling out with the love of your life is making up again. Here are a few ready-to-go messages to get your love life back on track.

[(xxx)]	A load of kisses
UWan2Tlk?	Do you want to talk?
PCB	Please call back
PCM	Please call me
NAH	Never again, honest
TMB	Text me back
UDNA	You didn't answer

HOT T🌶PS

There are several different approaches you can take to creating your own emoticons. The ones that you turn at 90 degree are usually face-on, however, you can also create side-on profiles. For example, '\\^U' could be a man with quiff and a goatee beard when viewed from the side, or perhaps O^W could be a man speaking with a forked tongue.

SrAU	I apologise unreservedly
IICO1OMLAIF	If I cut off one of my legs am I forgiven?
RNA	Ring no answer
WSLS	You win some, you lose some
IMstCU	I must see you
BMP	Believe me, please
IMsdU	I missed you
?:-(	I don't know what happened
:-|	Foot in mouth
:+(	Hurt

59

HOT T*I*PS

Another common approach to creating emoticons is to use a full-on face. For this you don't even need to turn the picture around. Here are some examples: '\=0-0=/' is someone wearing a pair of glasses. The best approach is to use open and close brackets for the sides of the face. You can then use a variety of punctuation marks to create the emotive effect. [^_^] is a smiley face, for example, and [>_<] makes for a pretty good angry face.

<G>	Huge grin
<L>	Laughter
<S>	Smiling
<W>	Wink
ICBW	I could be wrong
ITBE	I take back everything
My# 1	My number one
URT 1	You are the one
MstBLuv	Must be love
((()):**	Hugs and kisses

HldMeClse

Hold me close

LtsNtFiteAgn

Let's not fight again

URTLuvOvMyLif

You are the love of my life

ULiteUpMyLif

You light up my life

URTSnshnOfMyLif

You are the sunshine of my life

ILCUNMyDrms

I'll see you in my dreams

ILuvUMrThnWrdsCnSy

I love you more than words can say

LtsNvrPrt

Let's never part

IWLAlwysLuvU

I will always love you

LtsSty2gthr

Let's stay together

MlFrgvn?OKDrpM

Am I forgiven? OK, drop 'em!

U4Me4evr

You for me forever

:-) + (-: 4evr

You and me forever

TGlLuvWivU

This guy's/girl's in love with you

HPyNdng

61

Fun and games

You can't be together all the time, so here's a fun game for you play with your loved one in those dark moments when you're apart. It's called GUESS THE FACE.

{:^=|	Adolf Hitler
#:0+=	Betty Boop
((:=)x	Charlie Chaplin
{:<>	Daffy Duck
C8<]	Darth Vadar
:−) 8	Dolly Parton
:−)||?	Dr Who
5:−)	Elvis Presley
8)===;	Roadrunner
[:=|]	Frankenstein's monster
7:−)	Fred Flintstone
(:−)	Captain Jean Luc Picard
?:^[]	Jim Carrey
8(:−)	Mickey Mouse

:---)	Pinnochio
(II) F	RoboCop
*<I:-)	Santa Claus
3 :-)	Bart Simpson
(_8(I)	Homer Simpson
@@@@:-)	Marge Simpson
{8-*	Maggie Simpson
{8-)	Lisa Simpson
##O##	Scary Spice
>:-I	Mr Spock
(:=<	Star Wars stormtrooper
<I-)=	Fu Manchu
3:*>	Rudolf the Red-Nosed Reindeer
8:-[]	King Kong
:-)===	Arnold Schwarzeneggar
:-{}}	Commander Riker
:o)	Stimpy
=I:-)=	Uncle Sam
=)III)	Zorro
===:-D	Don King
:_(	Van Gogh

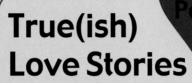

True(ish) Love Stories

Part 6

Cat and Brendan hadn't spoken in days. Brendan had sent her messages but got no reply. Things were looking bad, but he decided to give it one last shot.

B: PlsTlk2Me   (Please talk to me)

C: LMA   (Leave me alone)

C: :-| StL   (I'm not talking to you. Still)

B: Cmon   (Come on!)

B: IWsnt :------)   (I wasn't lying)

No response ...

B: SoSRy   (I'm so sorry)

Still no response ...

B: LO PCM   (Hello. Please call me)

C: ~~~:-| (*Still steaming*)

B: WCIS   (What can I say?)

C: FlwrsMghtHlp   (Flowers might help)

C: &Chclts   (And chocolates)

B: @}>-'-,---   (*Sends a rose*)

B: ChcltsNPrsn?   (Chocolates in person?)

C: OK ILF2I   (OK. I look forward to it)

B: ILuvU   (I love you)

C: 4evrBaB   (Forever, baby)